W9-BNV-209

Earthmates

Poems by Patricia Hubbell

Illustrations by Jean Cassels

MARSHALL CAVENDISH
NEW YORK

For Don and Shirley — P. H.

For Judy, Sam, and Annie,
my fuzzy fellow earthmates — J. C.

Acknowledgments

"Owl" first appeared in *Catch Me a Wind* by Patricia Hubbell, Atheneum, 1968.

"On Trying to Talk to a Frog," "Whales," "A Snail's Needs are Very Small," "Naming the Turtle," and "Flittermice" first appeared in *The Tigers Brought Pink Lemonade* by Patricia Hubbell, Atheneum, 1988.

Text copyright © 2000 by Patricia Hubbell. Illustrations copyright © 2000 by Jean Cassels.
All rights reserved.
Marshall Cavendish, 99 White Plains Road, Tarrytown, NY 10591

Library of Congress Cataloging-in-Publication Data
Hubbell, Patricia.
Earthmates: Poems / by Patricia Hubbell ; illustrations by Jean Cassels.
  p. cm.
Summary: A collection of poems about such animals as the shrew, crow, and minnow.
ISBN 0-7614-5062-9
1. Animals—Juvenile poetry. 2. Children's poetry, American. [1. Animals—Poetry 2. American Poetry.]
I. Cassels, Jean, ill. II. Title
PS3558.U22E2   1999   811'.54—dc21   99-039973

The text of this book is set in 13 point Meridien.
The illustrations are rendered in watercolors.
Printed in Hong Kong. First Edition.   6 5 4 3 2 1

Contents

Wren

Wren,
your name,
tippy
as your tail,
quick
as darting flight,
pert
as stripes,
is still
a brown round homey sound—
Come,
nest
in
my
poem.

The Phantom Fawn

Look!
There's a fawn
at the edge of the lawn
near the old bench
by the black birch!

When the wind blows
see the leaves part?
See those bright spots
on that beige mass?

But his mother is . . . where?
There! Where those branches hang thick . . .
        Oh! Now she's gone . . . .

And the fawn?
Where's the fawn?
Was there a fawn?
    Or just sun-dappled spots
at the edge of the lawn?

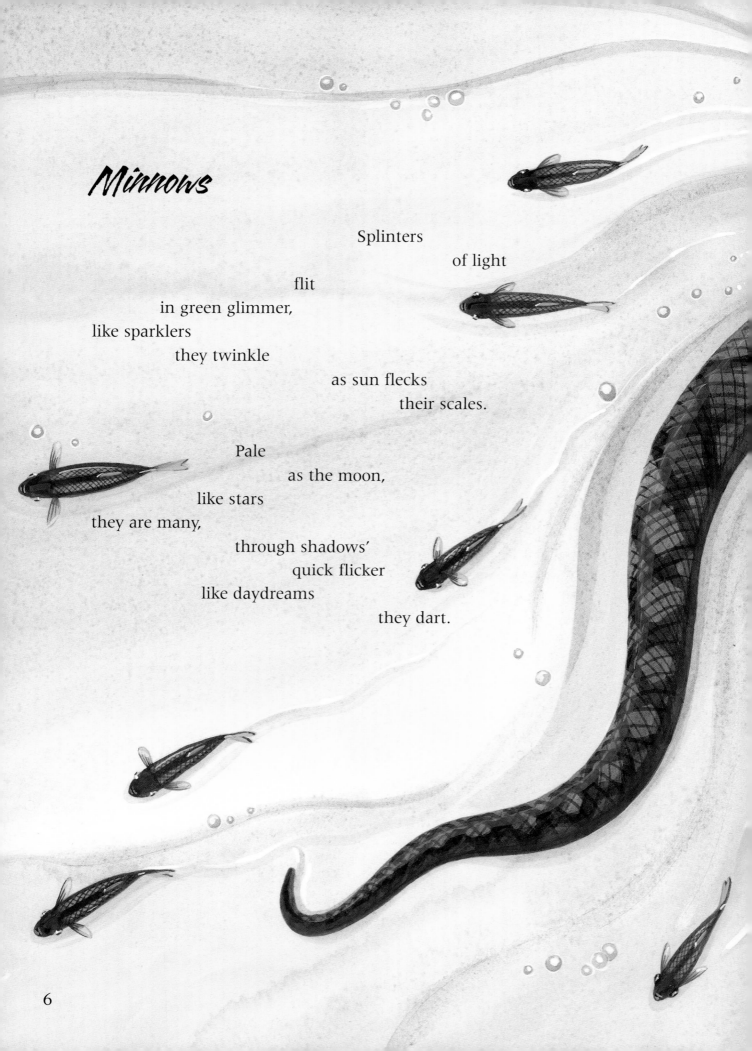

Minnows

Splinters
of light
flit
in green glimmer,
like sparklers
they twinkle
as sun flecks
their scales.

Pale
as the moon,
like stars
they are many,
through shadows'
quick flicker
like daydreams
they dart.

Water Snake

Cool
as
    pool,
    smooth
        as
            ooze,
            a
            twisting
        current
    when
he
    moves.
    All
        through
        the night
            his
            somber
            eye
        reflects
    a
    star
    up
        in
            the
                sky.

On Trying to Talk to a Frog

"Hey!
    greenglove
    O slicksleeve!

Stir-stump
my wet-skin,
my grabgnat, my
tape-tongue—

swim fast
my muck-love,
my leap boy,
my . . ."

"Brrump. Brruump. Bruuump."

7

Fireflies

sparklers

sparkling

glitters

glittering

and down in the grass, one pulsing chip from a shooting star. . . .

Shrew

There's
not
much
to
you,
shrew . . .
You're
definitely
not a lot . . .

Just a dot,
a small brown blot,
a tiny chunk of appetite
that roams the vast and wintery night
through moonlit dream
and midnight dread
pulling your footprint thread.

Flittermice

On leathery wings, the flittermice fly
　　across the starry August sky.
I watch from my porch as they wheel by.

They rush in a stream through the hay-mow door
　　of the old red barn near the sycamore,
to skim the pines and loop and soar.

Like little witches, they dodge and soar,
　　then circle the sycamore tree once more.
Four swerve back, through the wide barn door.

I watch the flittermice glide and swing
　　across the sky in their magic ring
and wonder how anything

wild as that
could ever be called by the plain name: "Bat."

Owl

"Who?
Who are you?
Who?"
　　"I am owl,
　　night's eyes,
　　wise beyond understanding."
"Who?
Who are you?
Who?"
　　"I am owl,
　　shadow of shadows,
　　owner of forests,
　　beautiful beyond comprehension."
"Who?
Who are you?
　Who?"
　　"I am owl,
　　plucker of moonbeams;
　　owl, most mysterious.
　　Beware."

Elephant at the Zoo

Penned,
he bulks
against the sky.
He does not charge.
I wonder . . . *Why?*

At the Zoo: Giraffes in Winter Quarters

We stand
in a landscape
of paint

Our blossom heads
nod
on their stems.

Below legs
like jointed
bamboo,

Our feet
root us deep
to fake earth—

Sunflower animals, we

Droop
in this shatterproof
vase.

Panda

The first man to see Panda couldn't believe his eyes.
The first woman to see Panda couldn't believe *her* eyes.
The first *panda* to see Panda couldn't believe *his* eyes.

God made Panda, her roly-poly and her colors.
He made black and white in the animal together.
He made fatness and small eyes.
He made polished nose and snub ears.
He made the smallness of Panda baby.
He made the bigness of Panda grown.
He made tasty delicate Bamboo for Panda to nibble.
He made Wind to blow through Bamboo,
                    to cool Panda
                        and to sing her songs.

When God finished making Panda
and saw her sitting by Bamboo, nibbling and listening,
He danced in glee.
He clapped His hands in glee.

Lion at the Zoo

In all that clatter
  only
    the great silence
      of his y   a   w   n . . . .

Auk

Osprey, loon, merganser, hawk—
    No bird that dives outdives the auk.
Auks zoom down deep through arctic seas
    To bring up fish as neat as you please.
Though their beaks are big, their singing's iffy.
    They live on islands bare and cliffy.
On chalky cliffs they boldly nest.
    On white-capped waves, they rest.

Mussels

A mussel doesn't hustle
As it moves across the sand—
Still, it uses all the energy
It has at its command
In wandering slowly up and down
The underwater dunes
And singing deep, unfathomable
Philosophic tunes.

A Snail's Needs Are Very Small

Sea-foam,
wet stone,
shell home.

These three
please me
mightily.

Whales

Whales are passing,
a pod of whales,
tail to snout.
They roll and arc
like waves riding upon waves.
They wear white lilies
in their blowholes.
The sun shivers
as they billow past.
I strain to hear their songs,
but the wind's fat fingers
plug my ears.

Sea Anemone

Down through shimmering green tide pools
   sunlight falls to minnow flash,
splinters to gold on pebbled jewels.

Starfish cling and snails creep
   over mussel shells' onyx swirls,
   over the gleam of moon-shell pearls.

Seaweed floats its tousled hair
   over a crevice, hidden, deep,
   where, in shadow, minnows sleep.

On crusted rock I kneel
   to see—
   one blossoming anemone.

Starfish

I hold you
in the stretch
of my fingers

little brother

in our fiveness
we are
one

Watching Fish

finswim tailsweep
  gill-gleam waterspout
   down down down
    lower lower
     and . . . *up*!
   weed-worn
   scale-skin,
  cool-pool
worm-watcher,
  fly-catcher,
   gnat-snatcher
    here, there . . . *now*!
   not . . . not, and, every . . .
  where?
leap leap ripple
gone!

Heart Surgery

The mouse is a kind of a man,
though so unlike (with his four
legs, his tail, his charming pink whiskers)
that he seems apart,
until you open him up.
See his heart,
soft and plump,
a tiny tangerine,
full of juices.
Each section
pulses with life,
drips with life.
Close him. Sew him up.
Like a man, he shakes awake,
touches a new day.

Moon-turtle

The moon
is a giant silver turtle
asleep on a black silk pillow

The turtle
is a small black moon
asleep in a shaft of silver light

Moon-turtle,
Turtle-moon—
your twinning
brings space and earth
together.

Winter Gulls

The beach is a cloud of gulls—
Gulls out to the breakwater
and farther than that,
a bumping of gulls
huddled shoulder to shoulder.
   Laughing gulls!
   Herring gulls!
   Ring-billed gulls!
   Great black-backed gulls!
All crowded into one
on the hulls of abandoned boats;
on rocks, on buoys, on driftwood, on floats,
gulls everywhere, a veil of torn lace—
     Or is it . . . no gulls at all—
     Just a thousand chunks
     of upended, shouldering,
     ice?

Gulls

Gulls
scold
tramp on sand
grab snacks
make tracks

Gulls
cry
crack clams
stand on stumps
check dumps

Gulls
brag
chase a wave
fly high
drip dry.

Barnacles

Stuck on stones,
glued to boats, clinging
to pilings, gripping rocks,
clamped to old oyster shells,
wedged in chinks, linked in chains,
scumbled in heaps—great
frostings of barnacles,
crusted together,
each in its
shell—

alone.

Rat

Rat:
The shout
of your name
slams through the barn—

You rattle the grain bin
scurry through hay
hightail it over the saddle rack.

Rat:
Those harsh consonants
that gagging "a"
the throaty disgust of your name—

In spite of it,
you are a wonder—
Flicking from the terrier
playing here-and-gone with the cat
scorning the baited trap.

The gray bullet of your body
shoots between hay bales
aiming for   *freedom.*

Crows

Crows
flying . . .

Or did a shadow
just

E   P L   O   D   E ?
  X

Wild Turkeys

Dust clouds hide red poppies,
    the snail bounces on his leaf—
        Wild turkeys strutting!

Naming the Turtle

Slowpod,
Weightlifter,
Housemover,
Homelover.

Seaflipper,
Rainstopper,
Pond-land-and-stream dweller.

Platepacker,
Boneback,
Hardshell
and Softhat.

Clicktoe
and Stare-eye,
Budhead
and Stemneck.

Nob-bob and
Lookslow,
Spotback
and Ridgetop.

Plod-plod
and Plopplop.

Logloving
Rockstone.

Birds

This is the town where the birds live.
(Twenty million of them by last count,
taken at the shopping plaza
one gray day in late November.)
You'd think birds
would be gone by then,
but there they were,
sitting on the high wires,
doing acrobatics,
tricking the shoppers into dropping their packages.
    Sparrows! Thrushes! Vireos! Jays!
    Robins! Cardinals! Hummingbirds! Chickadees!
    Wrens! Phoebes! Tanagers!
    The whole crew—
and above them,
teetering on the highest, thinnest wire,
singing sweet and flutey as Kiri Te Kanawa
one fat old mallard drake,
teaching us all
to do the impossible.

Earthworms

Freed by my shovel,
earthworms
show me
their acrobatics:

s o m ^e ^r s a u l t _s   b a c k f l ⁱ ^p ^s   t w i s t ^s

They wriggle in a riot of dreams—
How they will grow larger
than the pilot blacksnake
that loops in cool curves
over the apple branch;
how they will swerve and swing
across the lawn,
skein after skein,
rain-slick brown coats
stylish
as they dance.

Turtle Questions

Do turtles hide in their houses
and wish they were frogs?

Do they wish they could leap with a pop
from their logs?

Do they dream of frog-leaping
through pond, lake and bog?

Do they dream of high-vaulting
and green flash in air?

Do they tuck in their chins
and attempt chug-a-rums?

Or are they content to live slow, turtle lives,
with sunbaths and plopping
          and
             deep
               turtle
                 dives?

Chicks

The barnyard,
    spattered
        with yellow paint—
            My day-old chicks adventuring!

Geese in the Kitchen

The Canada geese have come into the kitchen!
For weeks, they have been getting bolder.
Now, they pad the linoleum,
check the cracks at the base of the stove,
study the shadows drawn by the African violet.

I scrape a carrot onto the floor,
toss chunks of wheat bread
under the chairs.
Their web feet make soft, familiar noises.

I turn to the sink,
run water,
imagine the geese
longing to swim.

But they have given up water.
They have entered wholeheartedly the world of my house.
They poke about the shining floor,
chuckling like children.

31

Summer Afternoon

A toad—
squatting
on my green rug!

Sun shining
toad squatting
blinking, smiling.

Through the open door
the afternoon breeze
shakes curtain shadows
over the toad
over the rug

and the little toad
suddenly
hops
out the door

squats
in scorched grass

debates
his next green move.